Blyton's™ TOYLAND™

BIG-EARS AND
CLEVER WHISKERS

This edition first published in Great Britain by HarperCollins Publishers Ltd in 1999

1 3 5 7 9 10 8 6 4 2

ISBN: 0 00 136124 4

Cover design and illustrations by County Studio

Printed and bound in Hong Kong

BIG-EARS AND CLEVER WHISKERS

Collins

An Imprint of HarperCollinsPublishers

It was a very blustery day in Toyland. Big-Ears could hear the wind howling outside Toadstool House.

"It would be a perfect day for drying my washing," he told Whiskers, his cat. "If only my washing line hadn't broken."

Then Big-Ears had an idea.

"I know," he said. "I'll go to the harbour shop to

buy some rope. Then I
can make a new
washing line and I'll
be able to dry my
washing after all."
"Miaow,"
whined
Whiskers.

"What's the matter?" Big-Ears asked. "Do you
want to come with me to the harbour?"
Whiskers purred and rubbed against Big-Ears' legs.
"Very well, you can come!" Big-Ears laughed.
"You like the harbour because of the fishing boats,
don't you? Or should I say the FISH?"

So Big-Ears fixed the basket to his bicycle and sat Whiskers inside. Then they set off.

When they arrived at the harbour, Big-Ears was almost blown off his bicycle. The wind was stronger than ever.

"You stay here, Whiskers," he ordered. "And if you're good, I'll buy you a fish for tea."

Whiskers licked her lips as Big-Ears went into the harbour shop to buy some rope.

PARP! PARP!

Suddenly, Noddy came driving along the quay. Beside him in his car were Tessie Bear and Bumpy-Dog.

"Hello, Whiskers!" Noddy called as they all jumped out of the car and walked towards the fish stall. "We've come to buy some fresh fish for our tea!"

Whiskers purred at Noddy as she watched
him go. She purred at Tessie Bear too.
But she didn't purr at Bumpy-Dog.
Instead she arched her
back and hissed.
She didn't like
Bumpy-Dog very
much.
Bumpy-Dog didn't
like Whiskers very much
either. He turned round and barked fiercely at her.
WOOF, WOOF!

Whiskers was so frightened that she ran along the quay and hid behind a lobster pot.

When Big-Ears came out of the shop, carrying his rope, he couldn't see Whiskers anywhere.

"Where are you, you naughty cat?" he shouted. "I want to get home before the wind gets any stronger. Come here, I say!"

Feeling very cross, Big-Ears put the rope into his bicycle basket and went to search for Whiskers.

First, he walked along to Noddy's car to see if Whiskers was hiding in there. But the car was empty.

Next, Big-Ears peered into Sammy Sailor's fishing boat. Was that Whiskers crouching down in there?

No, it was just a seagull. It made Big-Ears jump when it flapped its wings and flew away!

Big-Ears was getting more and more cross.

"Whiskers!" he shouted. "You're the naughtiest cat ever. And you certainly won't get a fish for your tea now!"

Noddy, Tessie Bear and Bumpy-Dog came walking towards Big-Ears. They had bought two plump fish from the fish stall and were now going back to Noddy's car.

"Why are you looking so cross, Big-Ears?" Noddy asked.

"Whiskers has run off!" Big-Ears grumbled. "Have you seen her anywhere?"

Before anyone could answer, a fierce gust of wind tore Tessie Bear's hat from her head. The wind was so strong that it carried the hat further and further along the quay.

"Oh, my beautiful hat!" cried Tessie. "Please try to catch it, someone, before it blows into the water!"

Big-Ears immediately leapt on to his bicycle.

"Don't worry, Tessie!" he cried, pedalling as fast as he could. "I will catch it for you!"

Big-Ears got closer and closer to the hat, but, just as he was about to grab it, it suddenly dropped down behind a lobster pot. Big-Ears saw the lobster pot just a little too late. He crashed right into it...

SPLASH!

Big-Ears was thrown over the top
of the bicycle and into the sea!

Suddenly, Whiskers ran out from her hiding place behind the lobster pot. Tessie Bear's hat had landed on her head, but all Whiskers cared about was Big-Ears.

As soon as she saw Big-Ears struggling in the water, she ran up to the crumpled bicycle and pulled the coil of rope, that Big-Ears had bought, out of the basket.

Then, with Tessie's hat still on her head, Whiskers quickly dragged the rope to Noddy.

Noddy immediately tossed one end of the rope into the water.

"Grab the end!" Noddy cried, as Big-Ears bobbed up and down.

As soon as Big-Ears had got a grip on the rope, Noddy and Tessie Bear tugged with all their might. Eventually, with a thud, they managed to pull Big-Ears up on to the quay beside them.

"Well done, Whiskers!" Big-Ears cried. "You saved me!"

"I think she should have one of these fish as a reward," Tessie said.

"No, both fish," Noddy laughed, as he removed the hat from Whiskers' head. "She didn't just save Big-Ears from the water. She saved Tessie Bear's hat as well!"

THE NODDY CLASSIC LIBRARY
by *Enid Blyton*™

Available in hardback
Published by HarperCollins